Dear Parent:
Your child's love of reading starts here!

Every child learns to read in a different way and at his or her own speed. Some go back and forth between reading levels and read favorite books again and again. Others read through each level in order. You can help your young reader improve and become more confident by encouraging his or her own interests and abilities. From books your child reads with you to the first books he or she reads alone, there are I Can Read Books for every stage of reading:

SHARED READING
Basic language, word repetition, and whimsical illustrations, ideal for sharing with your emergent reader

BEGINNING READING
Short sentences, familiar words, and simple concepts for children eager to read on their own

READING WITH HELP
Engaging stories, longer sentences, and language play for developing readers

READING ALONE
Complex plots, challenging vocabulary, and high-interest topics for the independent reader

ADVANCED READING
Short paragraphs, chapters, and exciting themes for the perfect bridge to chapter books

I Can Read Books have introduced children to the joy of reading since 1957. Featuring award-winning authors and illustrators and a fabulous cast of beloved characters, I Can Read Books set the standard for beginning readers.

A lifetime of discovery begins with the magical words "I Can Read!"

Visit www.icanread.com for information
on enriching your child's reading experience.

For Jim
—J.O'C.

For Nona and Emma,
who have me
under their spell
—B.S.

I Can Read Book® is a trademark of HarperCollins Publishers.

Lulu Goes to Witch School
Text copyright © 1987, 2013 by Jane O'Connor. Illustrations copyright © 2013 by Bella Sinclair. All rights reserved.
Manufactured in China. No part of this book may be used or reproduced in any manner whatsoever without written permission except in
the case of brief quotations embodied in critical articles and reviews. For information address HarperCollins Children's Books, a division
of HarperCollins Publishers, 195 Broadway, New York, NY 10007.
www.icanread.com

Library of Congress Cataloging-in-Publication Data is available.
ISBN 978-0-06-223351-6 (trade bdg.) — ISBN 978-0-06-223350-9 (pbk.)

20 SCP 15 14 13 12

Revised and updated edition, 2013

I Can Read!™

READING 2 WITH HELP

Lulu *Goes to* Witch School

by Jane O'Connor
illustrated by Bella Sinclair

HARPER

An Imprint of HarperCollinsPublishers

It was the first day of witch school.

Lulu Witch was happy and scared.

Lulu could not eat

her frosted snake flakes.

She felt as if bats

were inside her tummy.

Lulu got her new broom

and her Dracula lunch box.

Mama Witch kissed Lulu Witch.

Lulu walked to witch school

as fast as she could.

She did not want to be late.

A big witch stood outside school.

"Hello. I am Miss Slime," she said.

Miss Slime had a long nose

and a wart on her chin.

Miss Slime was very pretty.

Miss Slime took Lulu to her classroom
and showed Lulu her cubbyhole.

"You can put your broom
and your lunch box here,"
Miss Slime said.

Lulu sat down at a big table.

A little witch with curly hair

sat next to her.

"Hello. I am Lulu Witch," said Lulu.

"Hello. I am Sandy Witch,"

said the little witch with curly hair.

"Do you have your own magic wand?"

"No," said Lulu Witch.

"I do," said Sandy Witch.

"Do you have your own black cat?"

"Not yet," said Lulu Witch.

"I do," said Sandy Witch.

"Do you have your own broom?"
asked Lulu Witch.

"Of course," said Sandy Witch.

"I got my first broom

when I was three."

Miss Slime was standing

in front of the class.

So Lulu Witch and Sandy Witch

stopped talking.

First they sang a song called

"Happy Witches Are We."

Sandy Witch already knew the words.

Then they drew pictures.

Sandy Witch's picture was so good,

Miss Slime put it on the wall.

At snack time Sandy Witch got

to pass out the lizard cookies.

After that,

Miss Slime told the little witches

to get their brooms.

She was going to show them

how to fly.

Miss Slime and all the little witches

went out into the graveyard.

One by one the little witches

tried to fly on their brooms.

One little witch fell off right away.

One little witch bumped into a tree.

One little witch wobbled up and down.

At last it was Lulu's turn.

Up, up, up she flew.

She did not wobble.

She did not bump into anything.

She even flew backward

all the way down.

"Very good, Lulu!" said Miss Slime.

Lulu Witch smiled.

Miss Slime was proud of her!

Then it was Sandy Witch's turn.

Sandy Witch flew backward.

Sandy Witch flew upside down.

Sandy Witch flew in a loop-the-loop.

Sandy Witch even flew with no hands!

When Lulu Witch got home,

Mama Witch asked,

"How was witch school?"

"I like my teacher," said Lulu.

"But I do not like

one witch in my class.

She is the best at everything."

"Maybe you will like her

better tomorrow,"

said Mama Witch.

Lulu Witch did not like Sandy Witch
any better the next day.
At lunch Sandy Witch said,
"Your rat-liver sandwich
looks rotten."

"It does not," said Lulu Witch.

"It tastes good."

Sandy Witch held her nose.

Another little witch

held her nose too.

That night Mama Witch asked,

"How was school?"

"I still do not like that witch,"

said Lulu Witch.

"She is mean."

"Don't look so mad," said Mama Witch.

"Come and see."

"I made a new dress for you."

Mama Witch held up the dress.

It was gray with spiders on it.

"Thank you, Mama!" said Lulu Witch.

"I will wear it

to witch school tomorrow."

The next morning Miss Slime said,

"That is a very pretty dress."

"Thank you," said Lulu Witch.

Then Miss Slime told the class,

"Now I will teach you how to spell."

"Hooray!" cried the little witches.

Sandy Witch put up her hand.

"I can spell already," she said.

"Will you show the class?"

asked Miss Slime.

Sandy Witch stood up.

She got out her magic wand.

"First you close your eyes,"

said Sandy Witch.

"Then you wave your magic wand.

And then you say the magic words."

Sandy Witch looked right

at Lulu Witch.

Then she closed her eyes.

She waved her magic wand and said,

"Hocus-pocus watercress,

watch me change old Lulu's dress!"

All of a sudden Lulu Witch

felt something go POP!

She looked down at her new dress.

Oh no! Sandy Witch had changed

the spiders into flowers.

Her new dress looked so ugly now.

Miss Slime saw

that Lulu Witch was mad.

She made Sandy Witch change

the flowers back into spiders.

But Lulu was still mad.

"I can't stand that little witch,"

Lulu told her mother.

She wished she never had to see

Sandy Witch again.

The next day Lulu woke up.

Her head hurt. Her eyes did too.

She went to the mirror.

"Slippery snake guts!" she shouted.

There were big spots

all over her face.

Lulu ran to find Mama Witch.

"I bet that mean old Sandy Witch

put another spell on me."

"No, dear," said Mama Witch.

"I'm afraid you have lizard pox!

You cannot go to witch school today."

Mama Witch made Lulu Witch

get back into bed.

Lulu was glad.

Mama Witch brought Lulu Witch

a big bowl of dragon noodle soup.

It made Lulu feel better.

Mama Witch read

a nice scary story to her.

The next day, Lulu drew pictures

and did puzzles.

Was she glad not to see Sandy Witch!

The day after that, Lulu wanted

to fly her broom outside.

"No, dear," said Mama Witch.

"You must stay in the house."

"But there is nothing to do,"

Lulu Witch said.

She wondered what Miss Slime

and the little witches

were doing at witch school.

The next day, Mama Witch
let Lulu Witch go back
to witch school.
Lulu was happy.

Lulu walked to witch school
as fast as she could.

She knew Sandy Witch was going
to make fun of her spots.

So what?

If the other little witches laughed,

Lulu was going to laugh too!

"Welcome back!" said Miss Slime.

"We missed you."

Lulu sat down at a big table.

Where was Sandy Witch?

Lulu did not see her.

Then Sandy Witch came in the door.

There were spots all over her face!

"You had lizard pox!"

Lulu Witch and Sandy Witch shouted

at the same time.

"You look funny," said Sandy Witch.

"You do too," said Lulu Witch.

They both laughed.

"I bet I have more spots than you,"

said Sandy Witch.

"We will count and see,"

said Lulu Witch.

Lulu Witch counted the spots

on Sandy Witch's face.

There were sixty-seven.

Then Sandy Witch counted

Lulu's spots.

There were sixty-nine!

"You win," said Sandy Witch.

Lulu smiled.